Big Red Balloon

7

For Zachary
and Teddy

AF

For Si

KP

EGMONT
We bring stories to life

Book Band: Purple

First published in Great Britain 2012
by Egmont UK Ltd
239 Kensington High Street, London W8 6SA
Text copyright © Anne Fine 2012
Illustrations copyright © Kate Pankhurst 2012
The author and illustrator have asserted their moral rights.
ISBN 978 1 4052 5433 5
10 9 8 7 6 5 4 3 2 1
A CIP catalogue record for this title is available from the British Library.
Printed in Singapore.
47309/1

Big Red Balloon

Anne Fine

Kate Pankhurst

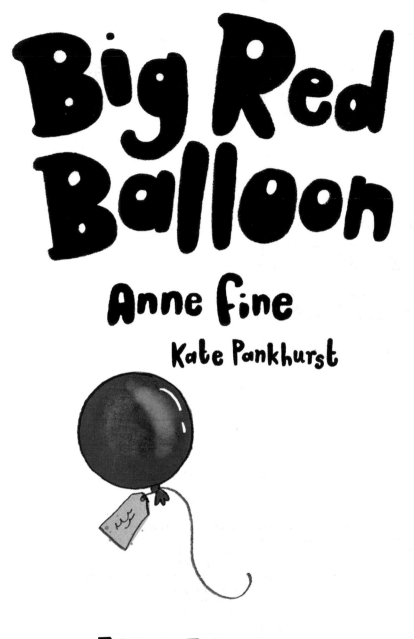

Blue Bananas

Last year, my school had a birthday.
It was a hundred years old. (That's
twice as old as my Nana.)

We had a big school party.
Every class was there, and all
the Mums and Dads and baby sisters
and brothers who could come.

We all went into the playground, where
there was cake and jelly and juice.

After we'd cleared away
the cups and bowls and spoons,
Mrs Dane and Miss Hall carried
out huge black bin bags that
had been hidden in the staffroom.

They were as big as floating elephants.

What was inside?

Balloons! Red helium balloons!

'These are the school's own birthday balloons,' said Mrs Dane. 'We're going to send them flying as far as they can go to tell the world about our special day.'

This one's for Pip!

We were all given a balloon, and each
one had a label with our own name
on it, and the school's address.

Mine said: **Pip Trent**

And on the other side was printed:

'Don't let them fly away yet!'

said Mrs Dane.

So we all held our balloon strings tight.
Some people tied their string around
a wrist to be even safer.

I tied mine around my arm rest.

Hold on
tight!

'Hang on!' warned Mrs Dane. 'Wait till I blow my whistle. Then we'll all let them go together, and it will make a good photo.'

Whoops!

I don't think Arif was holding tight enough because suddenly his balloon floated up – up and away – over the rooftops.

'It's very keen to get away!' he said.

'I bet it goes as far as France!'

'I hope mine goes somewhere exciting too,' said Helena.

'I hope mine doesn't get pecked by hungry seagulls,' said Jack.

Peep!

Mrs Dane put her whistle in her mouth and blew.

'Now!' everyone shouted. 'Let go now!'

The balloons floated up in the air in
a fat red crowd.

We watched as they spread out across
the wide, wide sky.

Some went higher than others.

16

Some went faster than others.

Some went a little to the side.

Further and further away.

Smaller and smaller.

I sat and watched them, wishing I could be like a balloon. I wished that I, too, could float over houses and trees and hills, going wherever I chose.

There they go!

We watched till we could hardly see them any more. They were just dots, like faraway birds all flying the same way across the sky.

Then we went back to our classrooms. Miss Hall fetched a map out of the cupboard. She drew a big black dot on it with a marker pen.

'This is exactly where our school is,' she told us. 'So each time someone's balloon label comes back to school, we'll stick a little flag on the map to show how far it went.'

George's balloon label came back first.
The man from the house across the
street brought it over when he came to
fetch his little Amanda from the nursery.

'It got stuck in my lilac tree,' he explained. 'And when I tried to poke it off with a stick, it popped.'

So George got to put in the first little flag on a pin, right by Miss Hall's black dot.

Surina's label came back next. She stuck in her flag. On Monday six more people in the class got to stick in their flag. Some were quite close to the dot, and some were a little further away.

And by the end of the next week, there were so many flags in the map that Arif said it looked as if it had flag chicken pox.

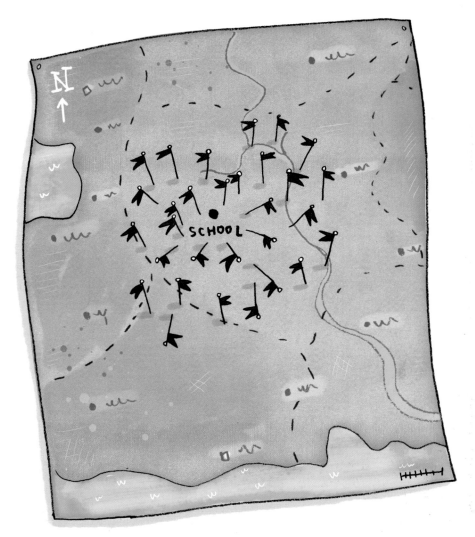

But my balloon label didn't come back.
I had to wait and wait, until I was the
only person in the class whose balloon
label hadn't come back yet.

Then, one day, Miss Hall came in,
very excited. She handed me a letter.
'This is for you,' she said.

'And your balloon must have had the
longest journey of them all – all the way
to London! – because the post mark on
this envelope says 'Buckingham Palace'.'

Pip Trent
Sunnyside Primary
Littleton Road
Puddleton, UK

'Is it from the Queen?' I asked.

(I was astonished.)

'I don't know,' said Miss Hall.

'Quick. Open it and see!'

I opened it carefully because I didn't want to tear the envelope. The letter said:

Dear Pip,

I found your balloon while I was walking in the palace garden. Would you like to come to tea, and see exactly where?

Underneath, she had signed her name in a really fancy way:

Elizabeth R

There was a phone number to ring.

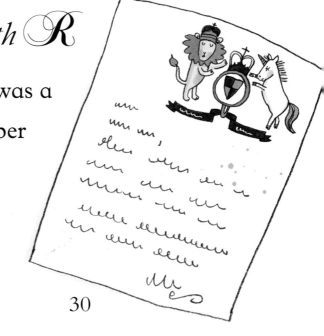

Mum didn't really believe it. Nor did Dad. But everyone who looked at the envelope said that the post mark looked real.

And everyone who looked at the notepaper said that the lion and unicorn stamp looked right.

So Mum and Dad tossed, and Dad lost, so he had to be brave and phone the number.
And I went to tea!

We took the van, and got there early, so we went for a walk in the park across from the palace.

I was really, really nervous. I couldn't even do what other people do when they are waiting to meet the Queen, like practise their bows or curtseys. I just had to sit being nervous.

It's almost time!

At last it was time. Dad showed our
passes to the policeman at the gate,
and then we went in and across the
courtyard. Even before we knocked, the
door opened as if by magic.

'Come in,' said a footman.

So in we went, up in the lift, and down the biggest widest corridor I've ever seen – miles bigger and wider than any corridors we have in school – with paintings on the walls in huge gold frames, and fancy furniture you'd never dare to touch.

Look at all the statues!

The Queen was sitting on a red sofa.
We all had a cup of tea, and then she
called one of her footmen to push me
across the lawns, so she could show me
where she found my red balloon.

Mum and Dad stayed in their fancy
chairs and carried on eating tiny, tiny
sandwiches with no crusts at all, and
little iced cakes.

But the corgis came with us, running round and round and round my chair so fast I was almost dizzy.

The Queen stopped beside a little lake. 'There!' she said, pointing. 'I saw a little flash of red between the reeds. I thought it might be a scrap of wool torn off one of my dogs' winter coats. But it was your balloon.'

'It floated a very, very long way,' I told her.

'Yes,' said the Queen. 'That is the thing about balloons. They can float free, wherever they choose.'

'Go anywhere they want,' I agreed.

She sighed. 'Not like people.'

She turned and looked at her enormous palace as if she'd suddenly been asked to mop the whole place, every single room, all by herself. She looked so sad.

Maybe, I thought, she never wanted to be a queen, at all. Maybe she wanted to be one of the things that I might be when I grow up.

A teacher or an artist.

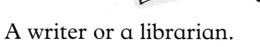

A writer or a librarian.

A lawyer or a doctor.

I tried to cheer her up. 'Never mind,' I told her. 'We might not float free like balloons. But at least we don't pop!'

'Yes,' she agreed. 'That's one good thing, isn't it? At least we don't pop!'

We both laughed as we imagined what it would look like if people popped.

Then we went back. Mum and
Dad were putting on their coats.
Someone had brought the van into the
courtyard. The footman who'd pushed
me round the garden waved goodbye,
and we were off.

At school next day I got to tell the class about my visit to the palace. Then Miss Dane handed me my little flag on a pin. She'd made a special one for me. It had a lion and a unicorn, so it looked royal.

Cool!

Everyone cheered as I pushed my special
flag into our map.

It was the last – but it had had the most
exciting time, and gone the furthest.

So had I.

Hooray!

Yay!